D1084001

Grace

Liesel Moak Skorpen

GRACE

Harper & Row, Publishers

NEW YORK

Library of Congress Cataloging in Publication Data
Skorpen, Liesel Moak.
  Grace.

  Summary: A cruel practical joke leads Sara, a lonely
sixth grader, into a secret, sometimes difficult, but
rewarding friendship with Grace, a proud old woman who
is afraid her daughter will put her into a nursing home.
  1. Children's stories, American. [1. Old age—
Fiction] I. Title.
PZ7.S62837Gr 1984   [Fic]   83-49472
ISBN 0-06-025798-9
ISBN 0-06-025799-7 (lib. bdg.)

Designed by Constance Fogler
1 2 3 4 5 6 7 8 9 10
First Edition

for Kate Armit Adams
a/k/a KAMS

Grace

Sara's mother is angry.

Sara's seen her angry before, but never like this. The look she gives Sara stings like a slap. Last night had been bad enough, but this is worse. Last night through it all— from the knock at the door until the policeman left, even after he left—her mother had been so calm. She'd put an arm around Sara while the policeman read her her rights, while he paced the living room asking questions, jotting down her answers. And when they left—the policeman and Amy drove off in the cruiser—Sara's mother had only said, very calmly, "You must promise me, Sara, never, never to do anything so cruel to anyone ever again." And when Sara had said very softly, "I won't, Mom, I'm sorry," her mother had only sighed and said Sara had better go on up now and try to get some sleep, almost as if she thought Sara was coming down with a cold or the flu or something.

But now, the next morning, she's furious.

She bangs her coffee mug on the counter. "I told you, didn't I? I warned you. But you wouldn't listen. You couldn't just leave her alone, could you? Could you?"

"No . . . I mean, yes . . . I mean, I'm sorry. I didn't mean to . . ."

Her mother snorts, as if she doesn't believe her. "You're sorry. That's wonderful. That will do us all a lot of good."

But she is sorry. She truly is. She'd give anything to take it all back. To close her eyes and open them and find herself back in the week before last and do it—or, rather, undo it—all over again. The part about not meaning to—that's more complicated. After all, they'd planned it, hadn't they? She and Amy, they did it pretty much as they'd planned it—only they hadn't planned on getting caught. All they'd ever meant to do was give the old biddy a scare.

"Don't waste your apologies on me," her mother says. "I'm not the one who needs them."

4

For several seconds it doesn't sink in. Sara drops her spoon in her cereal, splattering milk and cornflakes across the counter. She can't believe what she thinks her mother just said. She shakes her head.

"Never mind that," says her mother. "Like it or not, you're going to apologize to the person you harmed. You and Amy will march yourselves over and tell that poor old woman you're sorry and you will promise her that you will leave her in peace."

Sara winces.

"And you will promise me something, too, young lady. You will promise me that after you've made your apologies, you will never, never, under any circumstances whatsoever, set foot on that woman's property again."

"What if there's a fire and . . . ?"

"Don't be smart with me," her mother snaps.

"I promise," says Sara. She's not thinking fast enough. What has she just promised? She can't. She can't face Mrs. What's-her-face. "I can't," she says. "I mean, Amy won't. I know she won't."

"Perhaps not . . . but you will. I can't make Amy do anything. She's not my responsibility, thank God." Which shows just how angry Sara's mother is, because she's always liked Amy—Sara knows she has.

But her mother's rinsing out her mug and setting it on the rack as if it were all settled. Suddenly Sara feels very

5

tired—sick. Maybe she *is* coming down with something, something serious: a raging fever, hushed whispers in the hall, the doctor grave. "She's a very sick child— complete rest—we mustn't let anything upset her."

Her mother's looking for her car keys. She's late for work. "We're so disappointed in you," she says.

W hen did this nightmare begin?

With Amy?

No. Before.

If she needed to put the blame on someone, she might as well lay it on whoever came up with the bright idea of putting all grades six, seven, and eight in the whole district in one middle school.

Sara had gone to the same school with the same kids since kindergarten. She's known a lot of them since nursery school. Her best friends were Laura and Elizabeth. She had a thing for Roger Blakesley. That was a secret. A secret from everyone—except Laura and Elizabeth.

She hated the middle school. "Hate" wasn't the word for it. She despised it. She loathed it. She dreaded it with a dull, throbbing dread morning and evening. By Friday afternoon she was already dreading Monday morning.

GRACE

*

She waits for the bus on a corner, across from the old school. Hardly anyone in her neighborhood rides the bus in the morning. Their mothers or fathers drive them to school in the morning. Once in a while her mother takes her—once in a long while, if she's not already late for something else. Sara waits alone. On the playground little kids are running around, laughing, whispering, telling secrets.

It takes about twenty minutes by bus. Sara sits alone. Windows filmed over with road grease and grit—it's like looking through blind eyes. The bus gathers momentum as it rolls.

Once it broke down. Stalled, gasped, and expired just a couple of blocks from the old school. But there was no reprieve, no eleventh-hour pardon—only a short-lived stay of execution, until they delivered another bus. They weren't even late.

She hangs her coat in her locker. The smell makes her sick to her stomach. And the noise—voices shouting, giggling, shrill and deep; lockers slamming; even the blasts of radios, which aren't allowed. She can just imagine herself telling some six-foot eighth-grader with a mustache to turn his radio off or she'll report him to the principal. And then there's the bell for homeroom, like a scream. That's what she hates about this school—the racket and the stink. No, that's not it. It's the kids. The way they're always staring at her. Or the way they look around and over and through her. No, it's the way that everyone—everyone except a few losers . . . and Sara—seems to . . . The bell screams.

On the first day of school, Laura had stockings on and heels and so much eye shadow that at first Sara didn't know who she was. Elizabeth sat in the back of the bus with Roger Blakesley, blushing and giggling.

Sara tried.

She really tried.

She tried to dress like they did. But clothes that looked okay on the rack—clothes that looked sensational on Laura and Elizabeth and Angela and Jen—looked like a bad joke on Sara. And they made her so uncomfortable, as if she were pretending—as if she'd been cast in a play she'd never tried out for and given a part she hated and couldn't play.

She put the makeup in the trash, wrapped in newspaper so her mother wouldn't see it. She went back to her jeans and chamois shirts—and she scowled a lot to show she didn't give a damn what anybody thought.

Her hair was basically hopeless—too short to style much, or curl, or pin up, or pull back. She fried the ends with her mother's curling iron. After she washed it, it was shorter and stuck out behind her ears.

*

She's never been lonely before. Not really, and not for long. Not like this. On the bus she fights back tears—turning her face to the sightless windows. Never like this. In that big school with all those kids—all those kids except her and the other losers—who seemed to share some baffling secret.

She can't talk to her mother. She can, but she doesn't want to. She wants to, but she can't. Her mother doesn't listen anymore. Not like she used to when Sara was little. She listens, but she doesn't understand. She used to know what was the matter even when Sara didn't say anything. Even when Sara wasn't sure. Now she asks a lot of questions. She's always asking questions, but it feels to Sara as if she doesn't really want the answers. All she wants is to hear that everything's fine. So she won't have to worry.

"So tell me, honey, how's school this year?" Her mother's in a hurry.

"Okay, I guess."

"Just okay? Can't you do better than that? That brand-new building? And changing classes? I thought for sure you'd like it."

"I like it okay."

"Well, you don't seem very enthusiastic. What's wrong? Do you miss the old school?"

9

"No . . . yes . . . sometimes, I guess."

"Well, that's normal enough, I suppose. How's Laura liking it?"

"She likes it fine, I guess."

"You never seem to have her over anymore. How come?" She's trying to talk and put on her lipstick at the same time.

"I don't know. No reason. I have a lot of homework and stuff."

"Oh, well. Just so everything's okay."

"Everything's great."

A~my.~

Just after New Year's, on the tail of a nor'easter, in Amy blew—plunked herself down on the seat beside Sara, took a deep breath, and said, "Jeez, what a carload of creeps!"

Sara—startled—flashed a smile, turned quickly back to her dirty window, blushing.

"Catch that doll," Amy whispered, with a nod over her shoulder toward Laura. "All decked out for the Miss Priss of the Year Awards."

Sara covered her mouth to muffle a laugh that took her by surprise.

"So tell me, dahling, how's your love life? Don't you think Rajah there is an absolute dream? Why, the boy's a hunk of burnin' desirah." Sounding for all the world like Elizabeth at her worst.

Amy wore a black leather jacket with metal studs, skin-tight purple designer jeans, with black-and-pink cowboy boots. Her hair swung long and loose. Sara knew what the other kids would say. They'd say that she looked like a lowlife. Sara thought she looked spectacular.

They walked home from the bus stop together. Amy did most of the talking. They'd just moved in—from Massachusetts, from a medium-sized city—to the West. "It might be polluted and overrun with muggers and rapists," Amy said, "but at least it was alive and breathing. The best thing you could do for *this* burg," she said, "would be give it a decent burial." They'd moved into the old Chandler place—a derelict, gray Victorian that the kids had called, for as long as Sara could remember, "the haunted house." "Now that's brilliant," Amy said. "So inventive. So original. It blows me away." Her father—she called him Ted—was fixing it up. "Restoring it to its former hideousness." He was an architect or something. Her house was about halfway between the bus stop and Sara's—if you took the shortcut.

Ted hadn't gotten around to the gate yet. It hung twisted, half open, on a broken hinge.

"Do you have any brothers or sisters or anything?" Sara asked.

"A little brother. He's two. He just had a birthday." She looked away. "The housekeeper takes care of him."

"You're lucky . . . a housekeeper . . . I wish we had one."

"Yeah. I guess so. She does everything. All the yucky stuff." She turned her back to Sara. "Our mother's gone."

"I'm sorry," said Sara. And then, without thinking, "Did she die or something?"

"Nah, nothing like that. We should be so lucky. She just took off. Got bored with us or something. Some women just weren't meant to be mothers." She snorted—a half laugh. The corner of her mouth trembled. "I could care less," she said too loudly. "It's just the kid—Charlie—he's still just a baby, so he misses her. He keeps crying. . . . And there's Ted," she added after a heavy pause. "It just about broke his heart."

"I'm really sorry," Sara said weakly. "It must be awfully hard."

"No it's not," snapped Amy. "It's easy." She turned up her walk. "To tell you the truth, I like it a lot better. My mother's a witch." At the porch steps she hesitated. "Wait up, Sara," she called. "I'll dump these frigging books and walk you home."

Sara's block met Amy's at right angles. Where the streets intersected, as you faced the "pigpen," you had a choice of going left or right around the block to Sara's—not that it made much difference. Sara's house sat back to back with the "pigpen." So you did have another choice. It you dared, you could cut right across— that was the shortcut. A high fence divided the properties, but it had rotted out in several places.

Amy was still doing most of the talking. "Who wallows in that dump?" She nodded toward the "pigpen."

Sara laughed out loud. It was perfect. Not that everyone called it the "pigpen"—most of the kids did—but everyone agreed it was an eyesore. Ramshackle—what paint there was left peeling and flaking away, the chimney leaning away from the roof, which was leaning away from the chimney. The yard under sooty snow was a tangle of weeds and vines and decaying mounds of God knows what. In the thin, hard light of a January dusk, it looked even worse than it was. "Just an old sow," Sara said, thinking how clever she sounded. Amy was making her bold.

As if on cue, the door creaked open and a small, bent woman peered out, squinting as if the pale light hurt her eyes—as if she'd come out of a hole. "Scat," she screeched, flailing a frail arm. "I know you! I know you! Riffraff! Riffraff! Gutter trash and riffraff!" Amy giggled nervously. "Gutter trash! Riffraff!"

"She's always like that," Sara said. "She's always bellowing at something—at nothing. Nobody pays any attention to . . ."

But Amy wasn't listening. She was screaming back. "Shut up, you old pig. Shut up. Shut up." Starting up the walk toward her. But the head drew in like a turtle's, and the door slammed. "Old pig," yelled Amy.

Amy's new—old—house was being redecorated with antiques, except for Amy's room, which Amy was decorating in her own style. "Neopunk," said Amy. There were always workmen in the way. Amy liked to joke with them. She'd flirt with them and then say to Sara that they were "airheads" and "lowlifes."

Amy stretched out on her bed. Sara stretched out in a teak reclining chair. They played the radio, and listened to albums and tapes, and they talked. Talked until you'd think there'd be nothing more to say, but there always was. Once in a while the housekeeper would knock—

timidly—and ask Amy "to turn it down a little." And Amy would sigh and say she would, and she wouldn't.

They spent a lot of time talking about kids at school. They renamed almost everyone they knew and numbered them on a scale of ten. Laura became "Miss Priss"—a solid two. Elizabeth—"Oh, Golly Gush"—a three, barely. Jamie, who'd always been "plump," since nursery school—"Baby Fat"—a one. They had an argument— almost a fight—over Roger. Not over his name. That was easy. He was "Rajah, the Elephant Boy"—"Boy" for short. Over his number. Amy said he was a two and that was being generous. Sara swallowed hard and said he was a six. Amy looked at her hard and oddly, as if there was something the matter with her, but shrugged her shoulders, and they settled on four.

They, of course, were both tens—by strange coincidence, the only pair in the school to climb above a five. In the spirit of fair play they gave themselves nicknames, too. Amy was "Trash" and Sara "Riffraff."

Sara hadn't ever thought much about her room one way or another. If asked, she'd have probably said it was "okay" or "comfortable." Her mother called it "the badlands." When Sara started thinking about it, comparing it to Amy's, she decided it was basically boring. The funny thing was that Amy seemed to like it. When it was up to Amy—and usually it was—they went to Sara's. Amy

stretched out on Sara's bed. Sara arranged herself over
the upholstered chair (the fabric over the arm was worn
almost through and faded to a pale shade of drab)—it had
been her grandmother's. They played the radio. They
listened to albums and tapes, and they talked. And talked.
And talked. Nobody knocked to ask them to be quiet,
because Sara's mother wasn't home. She did interrupt,
though, by calling from the office a couple of times every
afternoon to see if everything was okay.

Sara's father was a doctor. His specialty was ortho-
pedics, which meant bones—which meant he treated bad
backs, mostly, and broken legs. Her mother was his nurse.
She had been a nurse before she had married—and before Sara was born—when Sara's chair still sat in her
grandmother's parlor.

Sara's mother hadn't wanted to go back to work.
"Against my better judgment," she kept saying.

"I'll just have to turn them away, then." Sara's father
sighed. "The battered, the broken, the hopelessly man-
gled." His office nurse had retired, and he hadn't been
able to find one who satisfied him.

"It's lucky you're a better doctor than you are a come-
dian," said Sara's mother crossly, but she smiled.

Sara's mother seemed to mind it much more than Sara
did. If Sara missed her mother sometimes—she had always been there, whenever Sara came home from

school—it was worth it not to have her asking a lot of questions and telling Sara things she already knew, as if she were a baby still.

So it was okay. But what if she left—not just for work, but for good? It made Sara dizzy just thinking of it.

"Do you ever . . . you know . . . like, miss your mother?" she asked Amy.

"Fat chance," Amy snapped.

"I guess I'd miss mine if . . . you know . . . she left."

"You don't know my mother," Amy said, turning the tape player up full blast.

Suddenly that school year, which had seemed as firm and as fixed and as immovable as a mountain, was rolling like a river toward its end. You could count the days down.

Sara was late. She'd overslept. She'd miss her bus.

"I called you," said her mother, "twice."

Maybe her mother had called her but not loud enough. Scooping up homework and books—no time for breakfast, not even juice. Not even a swallow of juice. She'd probably faint before lunch. She could see herself keeling over in the hall, between science and math—a very graceful faint, in slow motion, and into the outstretched arms of Roger Blakesley.

"Sara, what are you daydreaming about? You'll be late."

Out the back door. Dropping a book. Dropping two others picking that one up. Sideways through the fence. Her sweater catches on a nail and BANG! Her head. Something hit her over the head. Dizzy . . . not from hunger. Stars—like in the comics—spinning. Her books spilled over the ground, and her homework. Her science report, which was absolutely—and no excuses, no ifs, no ands, no buts—due today, fluttered away. All five pages—with graphs—floating like ashes over that old boneyard. And another thud—a broom—across her back, to send her sprawling very ungracefully.

"Please don't. . . . I'm sorry. . . . I was late. . . ." On her knees, trying to gather together what was left.

But the old woman wouldn't stop screeching, brandishing her broom. "Scat! Scat! Riffraff! Trash!" You'd have thought she'd been invaded by an army of Saras.

Mr. Perkins was unmoved by this sad story. He held the two torn, mud-splattered pages—the second and the fourth—held them at arm's length, as if he might catch something from them and said, sourly, "F."

*

"Damn it," said Amy on the bus. "It was a trap. She was waiting for you. It was a damn ambush."

Sara nodded, turning toward the window to hide tears. She didn't know if it was a trap or not. But she did know she was going to flunk sixth-grade science. And she did know her father would kill her.

"You were trespassing," said her mother, pursing her lips. She hated it when her mother pursed her lips. "You were trespassing, and you got what you deserved. How many times have I told you not to cut across that old woman's property?"

"I was late," said Sara. "You didn't call me."

"Twice," said her mother.

"I'm shocked," her father said, "and deeply disappointed."

He might as well have killed her.

Sara wanted to forget the whole thing. She talked to Mr. Perkins, and he finally agreed to let her do three extra reports in place of the missing one.

But Amy wanted revenge. "It's the principle of the thing," she said. "If you let people walk all over you, people will walk all over you."

Amy wanted to burn the house to the ground. Or drive a bulldozer into it. "We wouldn't need a big one," Amy said. "A garden tractor would knock that pile over."

Or nuke it. "It would be a public service," Amy said. "They'd probably pin medals on us or something."

Sara said it would be hard to nuke one house without nuking the whole neighborhood.

"Yeah," Amy said. "So much for the medals."

It was hard for Sara to think of something that Amy wouldn't laugh at. She'd suggested a humongous pizza order. She'd call it in. "Hello, Ye Olde Pizzeria," in a quivery little-old-lady voice. "Please deliver two dozen extra-large pizzas deluxe—double cheese and hold the anchovies."

But Amy laughed. She said she knew from experience that Ye Olde Pizzeria never delivered until they double-checked.

Sara's other suggestions—like a pin in the doorbell—Amy didn't bother to acknowledge.

"No," said Amy, suddenly serious—grimly serious. "What you and I are going to do is give that old sow-belly a little scare—give her something to think about."

Sara shivered, warm as it was. It was unseasonably warm for late spring. She hugged her father's wool jacket around her. It didn't really look much like a motorcycle jacket—even in the dark—and her Red Sox

cap made her look more like a Little Leaguer than a
Hell's Angel. Hell's Angel. She threw her shoulders back
and frowned—menacingly, she thought—at her neighbor's house.

The night before, they'd stuffed a note, pasted up
out of newsprint, in the mail slot. *Your number's up.
Hell's Angels.* That had been sort of fun—scary but
fun.

This was different. She shivered again. "Amy?"

An enormous cat—a ragged old tom with a notch in
its ear—leaped from the fence with a snarl and dove into
the bushes.

"Amy?"

"SHHH!"

Amy. Her leather jacket was perfect. She'd tied a red
bandanna around her neck. She wore a ski mask. She
had a flashlight and a tire chain in one hand and a small
tape recorder in the other. "I just wish this damn ski
mask didn't have these damn snowflakes on it. Do they
show? How do I look?" Pulling a stocking out of her
pocket for Sara.

"I don't know, Amy." She meant, I don't know if we
should do this. She was definitely losing her nerve. She
could feel it seeping out like sweat—sweating and shiver-
ing with the cold. "I don't know."

Amy knew. "Come on, Riffraff. Don't wimp out on me
now."

"But she's so . . . old. What if something happens? Like she has a heart attack or something?"

"So she has a heart attack and she dies. Who cares? Like you said, she's so old anyway. Come on, Riffraff. We can't stand around here all night jawing. Put the mask on."

Sara hesitated, but only for a moment. Whatever in her was struggling against this surrendered and ran. She pulled the stocking over her face and put her cap back on.

Amy smothered a giggle. "Outstanding," she said. "You should wear it all the time. Hey, kiddo, don't be such a worrywart." Slapping Sara on the back. "It's not as if we're going to hurt her or something. We're just going to shake her up a little. My God, Riffraff, the woman damn near killed you."

"Amy?"

But Amy had her by the arm and was pulling her ahead.

The house was pitch-dark. Not a sign of life.

They took their positions.

"One-two-three," Amy whispered. On three they began to pound and shout, rattling the windows.

"Hey, there, old sowbelly," Amy snarled, voice low, pounding so hard Sara thought the glass would shatter. "We're coming in after you. We're going to carve you up in bite-size pieces and feed you to the fish."

A light blinking on, by a bed.

The old woman sat up, looking around into the shadows.

"One-two-three," Amy growled, and they snapped their flashlights on, shining them over their masks. Amy rattled the chain. She switched the tape player on full blast, and from it came the sound of her father's old Chevy pickup with the missing muffler—on and off, on and off, just like cycles revving up.

She was out of bed, coming toward them, stumbling toward Sara. Sara, running, heard her fall.

"What if she's hurt? Really hurt? Like broke her neck or something?"

"Who cares? She had it coming."

"But we said . . . you said . . . we weren't going to hurt her—just scare her. What if she's hurt?"

"What if she is? She hurt herself. She should have stayed put. How did we hurt her? Did we drag her out of bed? Did we bash her with a broom? Is it our fault she can't stand on her own two feet?"

Amy started giggling. "Did you see the look on her ugly old puss?"

And Sara was giggling, too. It felt so strange—as if it were somebody else, as if she were just watching and somebody else were rolling in the grass with Amy and couldn't stop giggling.

She slept fitfully, woke to a sickening sense of dread. "Dear God, let it not have happened. Let it be just a bad dream." Sara saw her lying where they'd left her. Very still. Unconscious. Worse.

But . . . "Thank you, God. Thank you . . . thank you." No ambulance in front of her house. No hearse. She was standing there in her doorway, got up in a dirty old wrapper, leaning on a broom handle. "Perfect," Amy would say. "The old witch." She was calling for her cat.

That should have been the end of it. It would have, if only Sara'd kept her mouth shut.

Amy was late for lunch. Mrs. Baker had made her stay after social studies—something about a missing assignment. Sara carried her tray to the empty end of a table. She was just about to bite into a soggy tuna salad sandwich when Laura plunked a tray down beside her and said, "Hi."

"Hi."

Laura was concentrating on her milk carton as if it were a puzzle, as if it held a clue to buried treasure. "Where's your friend?"

"Amy? She had to talk to Mrs. Baker about something."

"Do you really like her?"

24

"Mrs. Baker? . . . I don't know. . . ."

"No, dummy . . . the juvenile delinquent . . . What's-her-face?"

"Yeah, I like her. She's my . . . friend." She'd almost said "best friend." Hesitated. Why? It was true, wasn't it?

"Well, nobody else does. Everyone says she's a lowlife."

"Then everyone's stupid. She's not a lowlife. She's just . . . Anyway, who cares what everyone says."

They ate—in silence. Sara's sandwich was worse than it looked. A couple of eighth-grade girls at the other end of the table were trying to eavesdrop while they ignored them.

"Hey, Sara?" Laura was working on her milk carton again. "Do you remember that time in the third grade—Mrs. McCune's room—when you and I and Elizabeth . . . ?"

They were off. As if they'd taken hands and stepped back in time—here and now dissolving, washing away. They were laughing—laughing so hard Sara almost slid off the bench. Before it was over—before the fifth-period bell brought them back and they had to run or they'd both be late—Sara had told the whole story. Amy . . . the old sow . . . the ambush . . . the note . . . the masks . . . the flashlights . . . the motorcycle sound effects. Laura was hysterical. She put an arm around Sara to keep from doubling up.

A couple of weeks later someone—some high school boys, as it turned out—threw a can of red paint on Mrs. Craig's porch. She'd called the police. She was hysterical, screaming for help. The police made a few phone calls and Laura—very much back in the here and now—was only too eager to repeat what Sara'd told her.

And so the policeman on Sara's doorstep about ten o'clock one evening.

"Sara, will you get that? It's probably Dad—can't find his key." Sara's dad was on call, so they didn't know when to expect him.

"Miss Roberts?" Looking down at his notebook. "Miss Sara Roberts?"

"Yes?"

A policeman. Amy in the shadows just beyond him, her eyes not meeting Sara's.

Amy sat down in Sara's father's chair, on the edge. Stiff, her jaw set, ashen.

When the policeman was satisfied that Sara had been home all evening, he snapped his book shut, saying, "Well, apparently you two aren't that old woman's only enemies."

Sara swallowed hard on the word. She'd never thought of herself as anyone's enemy—not since kindergarten, when she'd hated Roger Blakesley.

The policeman had launched into a lecture. He seemed to have it memorized. It was on respect for private property, on what it meant to have a record—"to follow you for the rest of your life," he said gravely. No doubt he meant to scare them, and he did, but he sounded so bored that the warning lost some of its punch.

"Do you young ladies understand what I'm saying to you?"

"Yes, sir," Sara whispered.

Amy nodded.

"Good, then." Shaking Sara's mother's hand, asking how the "Doc" was doing. He left. With Amy. He drove her home.

She heard her father turning into the driveway. He was late. His headlamps illuminated her wall, then her face— like a spotlight.

Then her mother's voice, thick and slow—she'd been crying—but gradually softening, settling. Her father interrupted, asking questions. Then a long silence.

Her father on the stairs. She'd rolled over, pulling the quilt around her, and slowed and steadied her breathing to the rhythm of sound sleep.

"You awake, Kitten?"

She didn't move.

"Rough times, huh?"

"Uh-huh."

"You okay?"

"I guess so."

"I guess I just don't understand this, Kitten. Your mother and I . . . That poor old woman . . . all alone there . . . Scared enough, I imagine, without you kids bedeviling her. Your mother says . . . you'll . . . She says you've promised her you'll leave the old lady alone."

"Yeah."

"That's a promise, then? Absolutely alone?"

"Yes, Dad." Her voice edged—with anger and guilt.

"Okay. You must be exhausted. Good night, then, Kitten. Sleep tight."

When she felt certain he'd gone, she slammed a fist in her pillow. "I'm not your kitten," she groaned.

"I know," he said softly, "but you used to be."

She was right—about Amy.

"No way," Amy snaps. "You can forget it. You won't catch me within fallout range of that dump. She's probably got a nuclear warhead by now." If that was supposed to be funny, Amy wasn't smiling. And as Sara turned away she said, "Why not invite your best little buddy-buddy Laura Priss Puss to tag along?"

"What if she has a gun or something?" says Sara. "What if it's another ambush?"

"That's nonsense, and you know it," says her mother. "She's not going to harm you. She might yell at you a little. God knows you deserve it. Come on. You may as well get it over with. I'm on my way to the office." She looks at her watch. "Come on. I'll race you to the corner."

"Good luck," says her mother as she leaves her. "See you later."

"I hope so," Sara says.

She toys briefly with the notion of waiting till her mother's out of sight and heading home. All that would take would be one small, gray lie. "Yes, Mom, I told her I was very sorry, and she said it was okay." Tempting, but even as she is thinking what she'd say, her feet—with a mind of their own—are delivering her to Mrs. Craig.

The paint has oozed and dripped down the shingles and the door, collecting in a puddle—scabbing over like a wound. Someone—the police or someone—should mop it up.

She taps, lightly. There, she thinks, it's over. I did it. It's not my fault she doesn't answer.

At which the old woman lets loose a howl that rises

and thins to a scream—inhuman, an animal cornered, trapped, dying.

"Well, tell us. How did it go, then? What did she say?" Her father puts his fork down. They're both staring at her.

"She didn't exactly say anything. She just sort of yelled. I tried, Dad. . . . It's not my fault if . . ."

"Not good enough, young lady."

"But, Dad, what am I supposed to do? I tried. I really did. But she was like . . . violent. . . . I'll bet you she's crazy. . . . Someone should lock her up before she really hurts somebody."

Her father puts his fist down on the table. Everything rattles. He's never done anything like that before. "I've heard enough of this. You, young lady, are going to apologize." He's standing up. "That's an order. No more excuses. You are going to let that poor old woman know that you're genuinely sorry for what you've done to her— that you mean her no further harm, that you will absolutely and without exception leave her now in peace. Do you understand me?"

"I guess so Dad, but . . ."

"As far as this matter's concerned, 'but' is no longer in your vocabulary. Tomorrow, Sara. Do it!"

*

30

Damn them. Damn them all. Her prissy mother hovering over her like she was some kind of retarded infant and then, "Oh, I'm late. I've got to run. Your father needs me!" Her fascist father—shouting out orders. Amy. Some friend Amy turned out to be! When the going gets tough, old Amy hits the highway. Just like her mother. And Laura. She'll get Laura. She'll pay her back one of these days. And that old pig. Someone should do her a favor and put her out of her misery. Okay. She'll do it. She'll knock on the door. She'll knock on the door and say, "Sorry I scared the pants off you, you old . . . you old . . . pig." She'll say it loud enough to raise the dead. And then she'll go home. And the hell with them. The hell with them all.

"Help."

It sounds like "help." Very faint. Sara's fist is raised to knock—to pound or tap, she isn't sure.

"Help . . . please . . . someone . . . help me."

She should get someone—her father, the police, a neighbor—someone.

"Oh, please . . . Oh, please." Sobbing. "Oh, please, God . . . Someone help me."

The door's locked.

Only sobbing now, no words—and fainter.

The other door—the back door—is ajar. It opens onto a small, cluttered—filthy—kitchen. The cat on the sink counter licking at a crusted pot, dives between her feet with a yowl and out as she edges through the door.

It's dark.

It smells of rotting food, cat sand, and worse.

"Oh, please . . . Oh, please . . . help me . . . help me . . ."

"Hello . . . Excuse me . . . Mrs. . . ." She can't remember the woman's name. "It's Sara. . . . Sara Roberts . . . from behind . . . Your neighbors . . . behind."

Silence.

"Are you okay?"

"Sara?" Very faintly. "Roberts?"

"Yes . . . from behind. Are you okay?"

The place is a shambles. Piles of old clothes. Bundles of paper. Unwashed dishes. Half-empty cans. One of the piles—a heap by the foot of the bed—moves.

It says, very softly, "I've fallen."

"I'll get someone. . . . My mother . . . She's a nurse. . . . My father . . ."

"*Oh, no you don't!*" The voice suddenly so strong that Sara thinks for a moment she's walked into a trap—another ambush. Only for a moment. The old woman's sobbing again. "They'll put me away. . . . They'll put me away. . . . Oh, please, God . . . Oh, please . . ."

"Don't," says Sara. "Don't try to move. You shouldn't move . . . in case something's broken."

"Here, lass. Give me your hand now. Nothing broken." She's breathing heavily. "Nothing broken. Just a wee hand. To me bed."

Sara knows she shouldn't but doesn't see how she can't, and so she does.

"Aye." The woman moans. "You see. Nothing's broken. No need running off to fetch some busybody." Her head sinks heavily on the pillow. She closes her eyes. The cat leaps from the shadows, curling in by her knees. She seems not to notice.

"Well . . . I have to go now." Sara's backing toward the open door. "I only came to say . . ." Her cheeks burn. "To say I'm sorry. . . . I mean about the other night . . ."

"Never mind that now," the old woman interrupts with a gesture that seems to shoo Sara away. But before Sara can decide whether it counts as an apology, the old woman is sitting up and saying, "Now where's my tea?"

"Tea?"

"Tea, lass. Are you deaf?"

"No, but . . ."

"No buts . . . I'll have me tea."

"But Mrs. . . . Craig . . ." She's nuts. A fruitcake. Babbling on about her tea as if Sara were her maid or something. "Mrs. Craig, I really think I should get my father. Dr. Roberts? He's an orthopedist—a bone man. . . ."

"Is he now? A bone man is he?" She lets loose an alarming cackle. "Well, we won't be needing him just yet. Not ready for the rag and bone man yet." And she's laughing until tears run down her cheeks.

"I'd better go."

"Not till you've fetched my tea, you won't. I'll not stand it!"

Sara rinses a rusted kettle and fills it. In case the apology wasn't good enough, she can say she made tea. That ought to satisfy them. She digs some dusty tea bags out from the corner of a cupboard.

The old woman takes the mug in both hands, sips, grimaces, says, "No sugar—you forgot the sugar—and you know I like it sweet."

While Sara's searching high and low for sugar, she calls after her. Whining. "And can I have a wee cookie with me tea? Is that too much to be asking?"

There's a little sugar stuck to the bottom of a bowl and a few cookies that the mice have nibbled at and left.

"You're not much of a cook, now, are you?" Sucking greedily at the tea. She puts a whole cookie in her mouth. "I'd be offering you some," she mumbles, "but there's not enough for company. Do you mind?"

"No, that's okay. I don't mind. In fact I have to go. . . . My mother . . . She's expecting me."

"Go, then . . . go . . ." With that same dismissive gesture. "Go . . . I said, and good riddance."

34

"Good-bye, then," says Sara—just to say something.

"Good-bye, then, and mind you're not late tomorrow. I'll not be made to wait here all afternoon for me cup. I'll not stand laziness, I won't. . . ."

Don't hold your breath, Sara thinks, stepping out into fresh air and sunlight.

"Well, I did it."

"What did you do, dear?" Her mother sounds tired. She frowns at a fistful of bills and junk mail.

"I did what you told me. I apologized to that old— to Mrs. Craig."

"Oh, that. That's good." Now she sounds bored. As if the whole thing had slipped her mind. "What did she say?"

"Not much. I think she's crazy. She told me to . . ."

"You're father's going to blow a gasket when he sees this phone bill."

"Anyway, I did it."

"I just hope you learned something from this."

Sara thinks, I learned to keep my mouth shut around so-called friends, and I learned to stay out of the path of batty old ladies. "I'm hungry, Mom," she says. "What's for supper?"

"Hello? Mrs. Craig?"

She was on her way home from school. Thinking about a paper she had to write and about what she'd fix for a snack and about how she felt about not going to the dance Friday night, and not thinking at all about old Mrs. Craig, when something brought her up short—stopped her in her tracks by Mrs. Craig's gate. As strong as it was, it wasn't very clear—not anything she saw or heard or smelled, like smoke. It was a feeling—a sense of something wrong. She stood there. Just stood. Unable to move. As if that feeling—heavy, in the pit of her stomach—held her down. For some reason she thought of a dream she sometimes had. A nightmare, really. She could see her mother clearly. So close she could almost touch her. But she called and she called and her mother didn't come. She couldn't hear her. What if . . . what if that old woman was lying on the floor? What if she's fallen again, but this time maybe broken something? What if she'd called for help and nobody heard her?

"Hello? Mrs. Craig? It's me. It's Sara. . . ."

The rear door isn't locked. Sara's hand is trembling. "Mrs. Craig?"

"Who's that?" Loud. And so sudden that Sara jumps.

"It's Sara. . . . Sara Roberts . . . I was here yesterday. . . . I was worried about you. . . ."

"You're late, Sara Roberts."

"I'm sorry, but . . ."

"Sorry are you? I was waiting. . . ." Her voice quivers.
"I was waiting . . . all afternoon. . . . I thought you forgot. . . . Here, lass." She pats the bed cover. "Come here
and sit with me a bit."

"Shall I make some tea?" She's relieved—so relieved
that it makes her light-headed.

"Aye, tea. Lovely. A cup of tea. And sugar," she calls
after Sara. "You won't forget the sugar?"

"I won't forget. I remember."

"Do you think me daft?" she says, setting her teacup
down and laughing—a light, girlish laugh. "Daft about
my cup of tea? Do you think me daft, Sara Roberts?"

"No," says Sara quickly and, to change the subject,
asks, "Have you lived all your life here? In this house?"

"Oh, no. Goodness no. I was raised on a farm. I was
raised on the big farm—my father's. . . ." She gestures toward the kitchen door. "Born and raised on my father's
farm . . . a long time ago now . . . so long ago. . . ." She's
dozed off. Sara takes the cup from her hand and sets it by
the sink. She's snoring softly.

Sara washes the cup in the warm water left from the

37

kettle, and while she's at it gathers up plates and cups
and saucers and bowls—pots and platters and frying
pans—and sets as much as will fit to soak. Behind the
cellar door she finds a broom—the broom that whacked
her? It's not much of a broom—worn to a fine point
but enough left of it to gather up some of the debris.

Sara opens the refrigerator. Closes it quickly. Opens
it again. She pours the sour milk down the drain. Scrapes
out some bowls so thick with scum and mold there's no
guessing what was once there.

"Da!" She sits bolt upright.

"Mrs. Craig? . . . It's Sara. . . . You were dreaming."

"Aye, Sara . . . only Sara." Sinking to the pillow, she
sighs deeply. "Only Sara Roberts."

"I have to go now."

Silence.

"I have to go . . . but I could come back maybe . . .
maybe tomorrow."

Silence.

Her hand's on the knob. "Okay, then, Mrs. Craig.
Good night. See you tomorrow."

"Grace."

"Excuse me?"

"Grace."

"I'm sorry. I don't understand."

"Grace. It's my name, lass. My name is Grace."

*

38

Going home—across the backyards—she hesitates by the fence, where she and Amy had rolled in the grass that night, giggling. For the first time she's sorry. Really sorry. And not because she's gotten in so much trouble. And not because the policeman or her parents had told her it was wrong. But because it was wrong. It was hard to explain. But she knew it was wrong.

Had anyone said in September that nothing lasts forever—that her sixth-grade year, like any year, must sooner or later be over—she wouldn't have believed it. But here she was, the last week of school. Of course they had to spoil it with exams.

Amy sits in the back of the bus with a gang of seventh graders. Sara doesn't know them. Everyone says they do drugs. Amy talks too much. And she laughs too loud.

She looks through Sara—as if she'd disappeared. Which for her I have, Sara thinks. For her I'm a zero now—or worse.

"Mrs. Craig? Grace? Hi. It's Sara. . . . I can't stay today. I have an exam tomorrow . . . in science. . . . I have to study."

She rolls over—away from Sara—toward the wall.

"Look. I brought you some stuff . . . stuff you were running out of. I stopped on my way home. Like milk and bread . . . and cookies. Look, Grace, I brought some cookies. . . . You were out."

Silence. A loud silence.

Sara makes tea. Butters some bread. Arranges it nicely with some cookies on a plate.

"Grace? Aren't you hungry? Don't you want your tea?"

Silence. Louder.

"I'll leave it for you, then—in case you change your mind. I've got to go . . . to study."

"What kind of cookies?"

"Chocolate grahams. They're my favorites."

"I hate them."

"Okay. I'm sorry. I really have to go now. I'll be back tomorrow."

"Promise?" Very faintly.

"Sure. I promise. It's my last exam. The last day of school. I'm through for the summer."

"Vacation? Already? I can't believe it. Where did the time go? Vacation? Now what am I going to do about you?"

"What's the matter, Mom?"

She had to be careful. If her mother got worried enough, she'd quit her job and be home all summer, sticking to Sara like a bad habit. And if she found out that Sara had broken her promise and was going over to Mrs. Craig's, she'd never wait for an explanation—even if Sara could explain it. She'd blow her top. And Sara would be grounded. Forever.

"It seems to have worked out pretty well so far . . . hasn't it? I mean my going back to work. . . . It's never been more than a couple of hours after school, and I call . . . check in with you. . . ."

"No, Mom. It's been fine."

"But now . . . How could it be summer vacation already?"

"Don't worry about me, Mom. I'll be fine."

"I meant to look into a program or something . . . or a camp. . . . How would you like that? A camp? Horseback riding? You'd like that, wouldn't you? You've always liked horses. . . ."

"No, Mom . . . I mean yes, I like horses but I don't want to go to camp—not this summer." She almost says she's sick of being bossed around, but she knows her mother will take it personally.

"But I can't help worrying about you, Sara. What if—"

"Nothing's going to happen, Mom. I'll be fine. I can help . . . with the house and stuff . . . with the garden. I can do the shopping for you."

"But . . ."

"And I'll check in . . . all the time . . . as much as you want."

"I don't know, Sara. I just can't help worrying. After the trouble . . . with the police . . ." She sighs, her voice tinged with lingering irritation.

"There won't be any more trouble, Mom. I promise."

"You won't set foot on old Mrs. Craig's property?"

"Mom . . . Why don't you trust me? I already promised, didn't I?"

"Sara, Sara, Sara. You were always such an easy child— even as a baby. You just never seemed to go through those stages—the terrible twos, the fearsome fours. I just never had to worry about you. But now . . . now I just don't understand you anymore. If it was up to me, I'd be home with you, just like I've always been, but . . ." Another heavy sigh. "But your father won't hear of it. He scolds me for being too protective. And he swears he can't find anyone else. He tried. He really did. He needs me."

"I understand, Mom. Dad's right. I wish you wouldn't worry about me. I'll be fine. I'll have a great summer. I promise. Just like always."

"Maybe you and Laura and Elizabeth could . . ."

"Sure . . . me and Laura and Elizabeth . . . We'll have a great summer . . . just like always."

Grace is sitting up in bed, ramrod-straight. Her jaw is set. Her eyes are fixed. Her arms are folded across her chest. "I'll not stand it, Sara Roberts," she says. "I'll not stand it! I am not a pauper, Sara Roberts. I am not a common pauper. And I'll not go abegging for my bread." She picks up an envelope from the night table. She shakes it at Sara. "I'll have no charity, Sara Roberts. I've money of me own." Pointing the envelope at Sara like an accusing finger. "Social Security it is, and it's mine. Not charity."

"I know," Sara says. "We learned about Social Security in school. It is yours. You earned it. It's not charity."

"Aye," says Grace, calmer. "So how much exactly am I owing you—for what you bought?"

"I don't know, exactly. It wasn't very much. A couple of dollars. It doesn't matter, really."

"It doesn't matter, doesn't it? Dollars and cents don't matter, do they? And begging? And borrowing? I suppose they don't matter, too. So you say, Sara Roberts, that I owe you a 'couple of dollars, exactly.' "

"I don't know. . . . Two dollars and forty-three cents . . . I think."

"Have you a receipt, then?"

43

"I don't know." She fumbles in her pockets. "I don't think so. I didn't think it mattered."

Sara's afraid she's about to begin again, but suddenly she seems exhausted. She slumps. Rubbing her forehead with her hand.

"You shall have your two dollars and forty-three cents, Sara Roberts, only . . ."

"What's the matter, Mrs. Craig? . . . Grace?"

"Only there's a trick. The trick is to turn this"—she holds up the envelope—"into dollars and cents."

"Oh, that's no trick," says Sara. "You just take it to the bank."

"Aye, the bank." She sighs and moves as if to get out of bed.

"But you can't, Grace. I mean, it's too far . . . and you're too tired today. I mean, it's not that important. It can wait till tomorrow."

"Aye," says Grace with an even deeper sigh, "but I'll not sleep a wink . . . not a wink until I've paid me debts." She's fumbling about for her slippers.

"Well I could go for you, I guess . . . if you want."

"Could you, now? Aye, I suppose you could." She has the check out. She's signing it, in a wavering script. "I suppose you could." As Sara reaches for it, she draws it back. "Now tell me the truth, Sara Roberts. Are you an honest lass?"

"Yes," says Sara, awkwardly.

"Are you the sort of a lass who takes what doesn't belong to her?"

"No."

"And do you tell lies?"

"No," Sara lies.

"Aye," says Grace, "then I suppose you could. . . . Sara Roberts?"

"Yes?"

"You might think to buy some cookies on your way. None of those nasty grahams, either. The nice chocolate kind with the icing on the inside. If it isn't too much trouble?"

"Okay."

"And Sara?"

"Yes."

"Save the receipt."

It turns out to be quite a bit of trouble. Not the cookies. Cashing the check.

The teller frowns. He frowns at the check, turning it over. He frowns at Sara. His frown deepens.

He will reach for the alarm—hidden under the counter. Screaming sirens. Swirling blue lights. *We know you. You're one of those juvenile delinquents who terrorize old ladies. And now you've stolen her check, have you? Book her, Bill.*

He's still frowning.

"It's my neighbor's. . . . She asked me . . . sort of a favor . . . She's old . . . and she's been ill." It doesn't sound very convincing. It sounds as if she's making it up as she goes.

"Wait right here a minute, miss. I'll be right back."

He's bent over a desk, whispering to someone—a manager?—nodding toward Sara, stalling, until the police . . .

"I know who you are," he says, smiling. "You're the Roberts girl, aren't you? Dr. Roberts' daughter. I thought I recognized you."

"Yes, Sara . . . Sara Roberts. She's our neighbor . . . Mrs. Craig. . . . She asked me . . ."

"No problem, Miss Roberts. No problem at all. Now, if you'll just sign here . . . Mrs. Barstan—she's my manager—she thought we ought to call your father. But I said that wasn't necessary—busy man, your father."

"Yes, he's very busy . . . all the time. . . . I always try not to bother him . . . because he's so busy."

"Tell your neighbor—Mrs. Craig—that she really ought to get her checks on direct deposit. Here, have her fill out this form. You can't be too careful these days . . . all the young thugs around."

"Yes . . . okay . . . I'll tell her." Stuffing the bills in her pocket. Trying not to seem in a hurry. What if they had called her father? Told him she was at the bank trying to cash Mrs. Craig's check? He'd probably have a stroke . . . or a heart attack. How would she ever explain—why she'd gone there in the first place, after she'd promised she wouldn't? They'd never understand it. She isn't so sure she understands herself.

Grace doesn't like the form the teller sent her. She wads it up and drops it in the basket. "Banks," she snorts. "Crooks is what they are, in business suits. Well, they'll not steal my checks, they won't."

She counts the money out slowly. Twice. Separating the bills into neat piles on the bedclothes.

She counts out the money for Sara. Two dollars and forty cents. "There aren't any pennies," she says. She holds up a nickel. "Now if I give you this, you'll be owing me two cents. And if I keep it, I'll be owing you three cents."

Sara shrugs her shoulders. "That's okay," she says. "It doesn't matter."

"Aye," she says. "It matters. Owing is owing." She hands Sara the nickel. "Now we're even," she says. "The two cents is for your trouble."

"Thank you," says Sara.

"You're welcome," says Grace, opening a cookie and licking the icing out.

*

At first Sara asks Grace questions just to be polite. To make conversation. To pass the time. But gradually she finds she is more and more interested in hearing how it was when Grace was little. Sara's always wanted to live on a farm. When she was little she'd badgered her father about it until he'd lost his temper. He'd told her he'd studied and worked hard all his life to get off a "damn farm," and he wasn't about to be dragged back now. She didn't understand. She'd even put a FOR SALE sign in their front yard.

"Tell me about the animals," says Sara. She's stirring the oatmeal. Scotch oats. Not rolled oats like her mother makes. Grace won't touch the "measly mush." Scotch oats for Grace. It took Sara three stops to find some—at the health food store—and it takes a long time to cook and it has to be stirred.

Grace is settled back in her bed—which Sara made while Grace used the commode. She hates the commode. "It's unnatural," she says. "It's back to me outhouse with me," she says, "just as soon as I've gathered me strength." The little house is neat and it's clean. This took Sara several days and a mountain of rags and a sea of soapy water. Grace doesn't seem to notice.

"Aye, the animals," says Grace wistfully.

"What kind of animals did you have?"

"Sheep. And cows—a few for milking. Chickens. A

spring pig or two. Aye, a proper farm me father's was. We cropped corn and hay and a garden—not your measly little turnip patch with some posies and a lettuce leaf or two. Nay, that was a proper garden. Grew all we could eat and put up and then some."

Sara isn't interested in vegetables. "Were there horses?"

"Horses? Aye, of course there were horses. It's not a proper farm if there aren't horses. Old Maudie and Zeke. Drafters. A team. None of your la-di-da lady's trotters. They earned their keep. Maudie and Zeke. But me Da sometimes would set me up on old Zeke's gray back. I'd meet them at the woods road coming home, and he'd bow and say, 'Madam, pleased to meet you. Can we offer you a wee lift?' " Laughing softly. "Up he'd heft me as if I were a feather, and he'd tell me I looked like a queen riding to her coronation."

"How about a dog? Did you have a dog?" This is a sore point for Sara. Her mother is allergic to dog hair.

"Are you daft, lass? Of course we had a dog. It's not a proper farm without a dog. We had lots of dogs—over the years. And not your la-di-da-di lady's lapdogs. Wee collies, most of them—to mind the sheep. Aye, we had dogs—and cats. Barn cats. House cats. The cats were me mother's. She had a way with cats."

"My mother hates cats."

"The McTavishes. That was their family name. Mc-

49

Tavish the First. McTavish the Second. McTavish the Third—now that was a cat—the Third was a proper cat."

"Is he a McTavish?" Sara points to the yellow tom cleaning its paw on the counter.

"Aye, he's the Tenth." With which the Tenth—as if he'd been called—leaps gracefully to the bed. He curls up, purring.

"Aye, she'd a way with cats, me mother. With cats and with flowers. Lilacs." She strokes the Tenth, who rolls to his back. "She planted lilacs everywhere. Every color and kind she could borrow or beg."

"Why didn't you stay there? On your father's farm?"

"Why, I married, of course. I grew up. And I married. Alex Craig. He popped the question. He was a good man. A dour man. But a good man. It's here he brought me. To this farm."

"This farm?"

"Aye, lass. This farm. This was a farm then, too. Oh, not so grand as Da's, but grand enough. This house—it was pretty then—a wee, white farmhouse, all tidy and trim. Barns. The big barn stood where your house is standing. Oh, we had acres of good land to crop. Acres and acres."

Sara closes her eyes and tries to imagine it. Acres and acres. No houses. No la-di-da-di lady's houses. No driveways. No lawns. No streets. No stores. Fields. Pastures. Gardens. Barns.

"Aye, and we lost it. Inch by inch. It slipped through our fingers. And never mind hard work. Oh, we were hard workers—Alex Craig and I. You might not imagine it now, but I was a strong little thing and not afraid of work. But never mind hard work. And never mind we took life as it came. Took it plain. Nothing fancy. Hard times. A bad year back to back with a worse one. He went to working at the mill—Alex Craig. He was a bitter man by then. And the harder times turned, the deeper he dropped. He took to drink. He died of it. Hard times, hard work, and drink. Right where you're sitting now. He fell over. Dead."

Sara stands up. "That's too bad," she says lamely.

"Aye," says Grace. "Too bad it was. Hard work, hard times, and drink."

They sit through a long silence.

"And now, Sara Roberts, would you do an old woman a wee kindness? Would you read to me, Sara Roberts? Me eyes aren't what they once were." She reaches for the Bible on her nightstand—its binding soft with time and wear, the gilt lettering almost gone. "Let's have a good, rousing one," says Grace. "Let's have Corinthians one, thirteen."

Sara finds the place. " 'Though I speak with the tongues of men and of angels, and have not charity, I am become as sounding brass, or a tinkling cymbal.' " She stumbles over the unfamiliar words. Grace catches her. She knows it by heart. " 'And now abideth faith, hope, charity, these three; but the greatest of these is charity.' "

"Aye." Grace sighs. "That's it. That's Corinthians one, thirteen."

Grace is perched on the edge of the bed trying to work her feet into a pair of ragged slippers. "Happy birthday," she says brightly.

"Thank you," says Sara.

"You're welcome."

"Only it's not . . . my birthday."

"Who said it was? It's mine."

"Is it? Really? Happy birthday."

"Thank you." She has one slipper on. She struggles to her feet. "I have to go."

"Where are you going?"

"I have to climb me mountain."

Sara giggles. "Your mountain? Really?"

"Get out of my way"—Grace snorts—"if all you can say is 'Really? Really?' I haven't the time or the strength for your nonsense. I have to climb me mountain. I always climb me mountain on me birthday."

"I didn't know you had a mountain."

"Of course you didn't know. I never told you."

"Tell me about your mountain," Sara says.

"Aye," says Grace. "I guess it wouldn't hurt. I have all day to do it." She sits down again with a sigh. Collapses, really. She's exhausted.

"Aye," she says, "me mountain. Me mountain me Da gave me. For me birthday."

"Is it around here?"

"Aye." She gestures toward the window. "Aye, you can see it there. Miller's Hill. That's what they call it. Them that don't know it's mine."

Sara knows it. Her scout troop climbed it once.

"There's a wee path," says Grace, "to the peak. At least there ought to be. Just a wee path."

"Tell me about it. Tell me about your father giving you Miller's Hill—I mean Miller's Mountain . . . your mountain, I mean."

"Aye," says Grace, but she doesn't go on. She drops the slipper. She looks much older suddenly and—the only word Sara can think of for it is "beaten," as if she were giving up after a long struggle.

"Tell me about your father, Grace. He must have been a very interesting person."

"Interesting? Aye, he was that." She chuckles softly, her eyes brightening a bit. "There's some say we Scots are a dour lot."

"What's dour?"

"Oh, it means grim . . . gloomy . . . never having a

smile . . . or a bit of fun. My mother was like that, I suppose. Though Lord knows she had cause. Three bonny bairns and only one lived through a winter, but me Da . . ." She smiles as if she were looking across a great distance . . . as if she would see him. "Me Da . . . as hard as he worked . . . as much as he lost . . . as little as he had to pin hopes on . . . me Da was never dour. He'd a twinkle about him . . . like a light . . . a wee, bright light . . . and nothing . . . nothing hard times brought him . . . could ever snuff that out." She sighs. And it seems to Sara as if her light were flickering.

"Tell me about your mountain."

"Aye . . . that would have been me birthday. I must have been about your age. That was the grandest birthday a lass ever had. And that was hard times, too. Drought. Seed lying lifeless in the dust. What dared to sprout just shriveling up under that murdering sun. Dust to dust." Grace has settled back in bed. Propped herself up on her pillow. "It would want every scrap they'd put away just to see us through. Skimping and saving. We Scots are good at that." She chuckles again softly. "Me mother warned me long before my birthday not to let me hopes up. Only a cake. Some stockings, maybe—mine were all darns, and them wearing thin. Da didn't say a word. He just rocked in his chair and sucked on his pipe. Not a word.

"Then it was my birthday. It was early. Pitch-black. He bent over me and whispered in me ear. Not to wake me mother. 'Grace,' he whispered. 'Happy birthday. Are you going to waste such a grand day in bed? Up with you now. And come with me. I've a wee surprise to show you.'

"He took me by the hand . . . to the hilltop. A bright morning—the sun slipping through the mist. We could see everything from there. Our farm . . . like in a story-book . . . so small . . . and tidy, and the animals grazing . . . like toys. And this farm. And the town. Oh, it wasn't really a town then. Only a crossroads then. He'd brought our breakfast with him . . . me Da. . . . He packed it on his back. Bread and jam and cheese. Hot chocolate in a jar. Aye, a proper feast it was, Sara Roberts. Fit for a princess . . . for a queen.

"And if that had been all, it would have been plenty, but he reached in his pocket . . . me Da . . . and out came . . ." Grace stops. She opens the drawer of the nightstand. "Out came this." It's a little gray velvety box. "This," she says drawing out a slender gold chain from which hangs a single pearl. "Come close, lass. Have a good look. See here on the clasp. Can you see it?" Sara can just barely make out a letter—"G."

"G," says Grace. "For 'Grace.' But not for me. For me Gran . . . me father's mother. It's her I was named for. Gone then. Many years. Before I was born. 'I was saving this,' said me Da, 'for your wedding day. But you know me. I was never the one for waiting.' And a good thing, too. The dear man didn't live to see me wed. He put it round me neck. 'It's a pearl of great price,' says me Da. And if that was all there was, it would have been plenty. But me Da says, 'While we're about this, I may as well give you this mountain—to go with the pearl. Mountains are grand for bringing things down to size.' That's what me Da said."

She runs a finger round and round the pearl. "A pearl of great price and a mountain to go with it. Afterward we always called it mine. Even me mother. 'Grace's mountain.' Did I say we danced?"

"No, I don't think so."

"Aye, we danced that day. It was wicked, me mother said. She said it was the devil's own game . . . dancing. But me Da took me in his arms and he whirled me around, singing. Singing loud enough to scare the devil. Oh, wasn't he a one for singing, too?" Her eyes brim over. "And for laughing. Did I say we sang?"

"No . . . Well, you said your dad . . ."

"Well, we did . . . me Da and me. 'Amazing Grace.' My song. He always said so. He picked me up in his arms. Big as I was. And we sang. 'Amazing Grace.' And an echo . . . I'll not forget it as long as I live . . . an echo . . . like an answer."

Sara thinks she knows where the farm must be, but she stops at a little store on a four corners to ask. The owner is pumping gas. His wife, behind the counter, shakes her head. "Craig, you say? No, I can't say I do. Sounds familiar. Can't quite place it."

"Mrs. Craig's her name now. I don't know what her name was then—her father's name—I don't think she said. . . . Her first name's Grace."

"Oh . . . Gracie McPherson, that's who you mean. . . . Gracie McPherson. It's the McPherson place you're after. . . ."

A young woman answers the bell. She doesn't look like a farmer or a farmer's wife. She has a scarf around her hair. And a paint-spattered smock. She smiles.

"Excuse me. . . . My name is Sara . . . Sara Roberts. I have this friend of mine . . . Grace . . . she used to live here when she was little." She manages awkwardly to explain why she's come.

"Well, of course you can, Sara. Help yourself. Take all you like. Can I give you a hand?"

"No . . . thank you . . . I'll be all right . . . thank you."

"You're very welcome. Anytime. And wish her a happy birthday for me."

She gathers such an armload in so many shades of violet, rose, and white that she has to wheel her bike home.

Grace can't speak. She shakes her head as if she doesn't believe her eyes. There are tears in her eyes.

Sara sets a big bunch on the dresser. And another at her bedside. "They're from your farm," she says shyly. "Your father's farm. They must be ones your mother planted."

"Aye," says Grace, still shaking her head.

Sara puts the whole box of candles on the cake. It's not a scratch cake—only a mix—she didn't have time, on account of the lilacs. "Happy birthday to you . . ." She carries the cake in from the kitchen. The little flames dancing, flickering—almost out.

"Good Lord, child! What's that sound coming from you? Have you taken sick?"

Sara blushes so deeply her ears throb. "I was singing . . . 'Happy Birthday' . . . only I can't . . . I'm sorry . . . I think I'm tone-deaf."

"Stuff and nonsense," snorts Grace. "Of course you

can. Do you think our Lord gave the gift of song to the wee birds and not to you?"

Sara thinks, But I can't fly either, but doesn't say so.

"Let's give it another go," says Grace.

"I can't."

"Can't, lass? Can't try?"

"No . . . yes . . . I can't sing. I can't."

"Aye, but you can try, can't you?"

Very faintly. Hardly a whisper. "Happy birth . . ."

Grace puts her hands over her ears, slowly shaking her head. "Tone-deaf, you say? Aye, well, we can't leave everything to the dear Lord, can we? I'll have to teach you singing myself."

That settled to her satisfaction, she has two large slices of cake and most of a small one. Enjoying every bite. Smacking her lips.

But a little later—Sara's washed up and is getting ready to go and trying to think what she'll say to her mother, how she'll explain where she's been—there are tears again in Grace's eyes.

"Grace?"

"Aye."

"Is something wrong?"

"Aye."

"What's wrong?"

"I'm afraid."

"What are you afraid of, Grace? Don't be afraid." A

wave of guilt washes over her. On account of what she and Amy had done.

Grace is sobbing softly. "I'm afraid they'll find out . . . about me . . . and . . . they'll put me away."

"Who? Put you away? Where? Where would they put you?"

"I'm too old . . . and too weak . . . can hardly stand up anymore . . . you've seen it . . . and sometimes . . . sometimes I forget things . . . I get mixed up in my head . . . and they'll say . . . I can't take care of myself, and they'll lock me away. . . . Oh, they'll call it a 'home' . . . but for all that it'll be a prison . . . with locks and keys . . . a prison for us too old to stand up and not old enough to lie down and die."

"But they won't. Nobody knows. Nobody knows about you but me."

"And you won't tell? You'll keep it a secret? You'll not tell on me, then?"

"No, I won't tell anyone. Why would I?"

"Promise?"

"Yes, I promise."

"And you'll help me? Do for me what I can't do?" She's sobbing again. "Oh, please . . . please don't let them lock me away. All I ask is to die in my bed. Oh, please, God. Please."

Sara takes her hand and holds it tight. "I'll help," she says, "and I won't tell. I promise." With a sinking feeling, though, as if she were swimming out beyond her depth. If she did tell her parents about Grace, they'd know she had broken her promise to them—to stay away from Grace—and how could she explain how it had happened, and how could she bear it if they looked at her again as if she were some nasty crawling thing they'd like to step on, and what would they do about Grace? They'd probably have her put in a home. . . . Probably they'd have to, and that would probably kill Grace . . . and it would be her fault. Promises. Too many. She's dizzy and sick to her stomach.

The sobbing slowly softens. And stops. She's asleep. And it's too late now. Sara's promised.

"I've been worried sick! Where have you been all this time?" Her mother is angry. Almost as angry as she was that morning after.

"I'm sorry. I rode my bike . . . out to the country. . . . I got a flat."

"All by yourself?"

"No . . . with a bunch of kids."

"Who?"

"Just kids . . . Laura . . . Elizabeth . . . you know."

"No, I don't know. What I do know is that I've been sitting here wondering if I should call the police. You might have had the courtesy to call me."

"I'm sorry. I'm really sorry. I was . . . we were way out

in the country. There wasn't any phone. It won't happen again, Mom. I promise."

"I certainly hope not," says her mother grimly.

In the morning Grace is again perched on the edge of the bed waiting—impatiently. Sara's late.

"I'm sorry." She seems to be always saying "I'm sorry" lately. "I had to wait for my dad to leave. . . . He overslept. . . . He was on call last night."

"Rubbish. Never mind it. I've been waiting for you for hours. I mean to take some exercise."

"Exercise?"

"That's what I said, lass. Exercise."

Sara tries to picture Grace doing sit-ups or push-ups, or jogging around the block. "But you can't, Grace. How can you?"

"I can," she says with a stubborn set of her jaw, "because I mean to. I mean to get me strength back."

"What kind of exercise do you mean?"

"Walking will do . . . to start with. A few steps today. Tomorrow a few more. And by and by. Aye, you'll see."

She leans heavily on Sara's arm. A step. Another. Grace bites her lip. Another . . . half a step. She moans.

"Isn't that enough?" Sara says. "For now, I mean."

Another. "Aye," she says faintly, "for now."

As soon as she's back in bed she sleeps—exhausted.

O ne morning—"Helen? Helen?" Her voice rising, sharp and thin, as if angry, or afraid. "Helen . . . I know it's you. . . . Is that you, Helen?"

"No . . . it's Sara. Who's Helen?"

"Oh, it's only Sara Roberts." With a sigh. "It's only Sara Roberts."

After breakfast she tries again. "Who's Helen?"

"Helen? Helen who?"

"That's what I'm asking. The Helen you thought I was when I came in this morning."

"Oh, that Helen. That's nobody."

"Nobody?"

"Aye. Nobody you'd know." After a long pause, "My daughter."

"I didn't know you had any children."

"I don't."

"But didn't you just say you did?"

"Aye. I suppose I did. But she's not a child. I don't remember that she ever was one." Grace snorts. "She's a businesswoman, Helen is."

"Where does she live?"

"Nowhere. I don't know. Somewhere. I never could remember. Halfway around the world somewhere." She's fumbling through her drawer. She finds a small address book and tosses it toward Sara as if throwing it away.

Sara leafs through dog-eared pages. "Is her name Craig?"

"Of course her name is Craig, you ninny. What did you think her name was? Rockefeller?"

"I just thought she might be married . . . or something."

"Married? Helen? Very unlikely."

Sara finds it: Helen Craig, 31 East Park, Apt. #25, San Francisco, California.

"Since you brought it up," says Grace, "I think we best drop a wee line to Helen. Just so she doesn't fly in on her broomstick—sticking her great nose in nobody's business. Aye. Pen and paper, lass, and put it down just as I say it. *Dear Helen . . .*"

Dear Helen, Sara writes.

"My nurse is writing this for me. . . ."

Sara looks up.

"Oh, don't be such a damn Goody Two-shoes," snorts Grace with a dismissing wave. "Such a wee lie." She measures it with thumb and forefinger barely spread. "Such a wee lie. For aren't you that, really—almost like a nurse? And only for Helen's sake, too? So she'll feel better? And stay put—in whatever godforsaken spot she lit. We'll all feel better for that." Triumphantly. "Now you tell me, lass, whoever's the worse for it?"

In her mind's eye Sara can see the great big-beaked, businesslike Helen descending upon them.

"Well, get on with it, then, lass. Say: *I'm just grand. Fit as a fiddle. Not to worry.* Underline that. *Not to worry. I see the doctor regularly.*" Sara hesitates. "Go on. Get on with it, then. *He says I'll live to be a hundred.* No, wait a bit. Change that to *she. She says I'll live to be a hundred.* Aye. Helen will like that. Good. I'll sign it."

"Shall I put 'Love'?"

"Never mind that. Suit yourself."

Sara puts *Love.* Grace signs it. The envelope is sealed. Addressed. A dusty stamp is found in the back of the drawer. The letter's dropped in the box on the corner. It disappears.

There's no reply.

Voices drifting up the stairs. Soft. Steady. Her mother laughs.

It's been a bad day. Grace was grumpy and confused. She complained about everything. She whimpered. She whined. She said Sara was stealing her blind. She said Sara hurt her—on purpose. She said she hadn't seen Sara in weeks. And when Sara went outside for a few minutes, she couldn't remember who she was. She was getting worse. Some days she seemed a little better. But week by week she was getting worse.

Her mother, laughing gently, says her name.

If she went down to them . . . if she told them what was happening, they'd listen—they always listened—and they'd understand. She could tell them about Helen. She could give them her address. They'd know what to do. Would they? What if something awful happened? What if Grace died? She could hear her father. *"If only you hadn't lied. We might have saved her. What you've done is criminal. You might as well have murdered the poor old woman."*

And if they put Grace away? If they shut her away in some old ladies' 'home' . . . She could see the look in Grace's eyes. It would kill her. Sara's sure of it.

When she was little, it had all seemed so simple. Right and wrong. Lying was wrong. Stealing was wrong. Breaking promises was wrong. When did it get so complicated? She wants to do what's right. But how? Someone should tell her what to do. But who?

It's so unfair. She buries her face in her pillow and sobs herself to sleep. She dreams she is on a mountaintop looking down on a farm. Her farm. Horses. Her horses. Galloping. Galloping.

Sara's surprised to find her father at breakfast. Usually he's gone before she's up.

"Hi," he says, looking up from a medical journal. He seems uncomfortable—embarrassed. As if there were something he didn't want to say.

"Hi, Dad." She slices a banana on her cereal.

"Your father and I would like to talk to you." Her mother seems embarrassed, too.

Sara concentrates on her cereal.

"Sara, dear," says her mother finally, "is everything all right?"

"Sure. Everything's fine."

"I mean . . . we mean . . . it's such a strange summer for you. I mean . . . if I could be home . . . you seem to be . . . alone so much."

"It's okay. I don't mind. I keep busy. I'm fine. Really."

"And you're not . . ." Now her mother sounds really uncomfortable. And her father's looking out the window. "I mean . . . you're not in any sort of . . . trouble, are you?"

Sara pushes her chair back so abruptly it nearly tips over. "Of course I'm not in any trouble. Don't you trust me? What do you think I'm doing? Terrorizing the neighborhood? Dealing drugs? Who do you think I am? Public enemy number one?"

Her mother looks as if she's about to cry. "There's no need to take that tone," she says. "We only wanted to help."

"Hey, Sara," her father interrupts. "How about making rounds with me this morning? I hardly get a chance to see you these days . . . and before I know what's hit me, you'll be all grown up and married to some movie star or Greek shipping magnate, and then all I'll see is your picture in the tabloids."

"Oh, Daddy."

"Come on, Kitten. Be a sport. You used to love making rounds."

There's just time enough while her father shaves to dash across the yard. She puts a jar of peanut butter and some crackers on the nightstand with a butter knife. "I'm sorry," she says. "I've got to go. I'll be back in a jiffy."

Grace rolls away. She isn't speaking.

She follows him. At a distance. Dragging her feet. Stopping to study some dumb thing—a poster about what smoking does to your lungs—because it's so embarrassing.

When she was little she walked beside him, holding his hand, and yes—she loved it. It felt as if he were the sun and she was warm and glowing in his light. Everyone loved him. The nurses. The orderlies. The patients. And because she was his, they loved her, too. They'd make such a fuss over her. Mrs. Nelson, who had been the head nurse on the orthopedic wing forever—who was famous for being hard as nails and sharp as a tack—would lift her up on the nurses' station and give her one fat chocolate from the box she kept under lock and key. She'd always say Sara was "her little princess." And the patients—even some of the very sick ones, just up from surgery—would smile and nod when they saw her. "Is this little beauty yours, Doc?"

"She sure is. Mr. So-and-so, meet Sara—the light of my life."

Her father's talking to Mrs. Nelson. In a low voice. He studies one of the metallic charts, making notes.

From one of the rooms around the nurses' station a woman cries out: "Mama! Mama! Help me, Mama!"

Sara can see from where she's standing through the half-open door. It's a double room, but one bed's empty. The woman in the other bed is restrained. That's hospital talk for saying her wrists are strapped to the bed frame—for her own protection, of course. She isn't a very dangerous-looking woman. She can't weigh a hundred pounds. She rocks from side to side tugging at the leather bracelets. Crying and moaning. "Oh, Mama, Mama . . . Mama . . ."

She stops. Suddenly. She's very still. Hearing or seeing or sensing Sara near the door. Her voice is shrill. It seems to reach toward Sara like a hand. "Mama! Mama! Is it you? Oh, please, Mama, take me home now. I won't be naughty anymore. I'll be your good girl, Mama. I'm sorry, Mama. I'll be good.

Sara backs away.

The woman screams. An animal scream. Sara winces. She wants to cover her ears but can't with her father and Mrs. Nelson watching.

Mrs. Nelson sighs. Steps out from behind the nurses' station. Slowly. Deliberately. "Now, Sadie, you're to stop that fussing." She goes into the room. "You're in the hospital. You're going home tomorrow—if you're a good girl. But you must stop the noise. You'll just upset the other girls."

On the way home Sara asks, "Is she really going home tomorrow?"

"Who's that?"

"That old woman. The one who was crying."

"Yes, she's doing very well. She'll be going back to the nursing home."

"What's the matter with her?"

"She broke her hip. That's a common injury for someone her age, but a very serious one. Quite a few old people die of it—from the complications. But Sadie's amazing. Healing much faster than I expected."

"Is she always like that? So unhappy?"

"No. She does better in the home. Hospitals aren't

70

good places for old people. Most of them do better at home."

"I thought hospitals were supposed to make you better."

He laughs. Reaches over to pat her leg. "Well, that's the idea, Kitten. And sometimes that's the way it works."

"What if nothing's the matter with someone except they're old . . . and weak? Would it do any good to send them to a hospital?"

"Well, that depends. I like to keep my patients at home if possible. If there's someone looking after them. Old age isn't a disease—like the measles. Sometimes we can make it more comfortable, but people don't get over it. They just get older."

Sara is silent.

"You're pretty young, Kitten, to be brooding about old age and death."

"I'm not brooding," Sara says. "Just wondering was all."

G race is lying exactly as she'd left her. With her back to Sara. "Hi. Can I get you something? Tea? Cookies or something?"

Silence.

"How about a Twinkie?"

Grace rolls over. Facing Sara. She's been crying. "I don't want a Twinkie," she says. "I don't want a cookie. I don't want any damn crackers." With a glance filled with disgust toward the unopened box. "I don't want any damn peanut butter for breakfast. I've never had any damn peanut butter for me damn breakfast. I want me damn breakfast."

"Breakfast?" Sara glances at her watch. "It's pretty late for breakfast.

"Breakfast," says Grace. "And by the way, I may be old. And I may be feeble. And sometimes things may slip me mind. But I do know what a jiffy is. That was not a jiffy."

"I'm sorry. I got tied up."

"Humph," says Grace.

She makes oatmeal.

"Raw," says Grace, pushing it away. Sara spoons it back into the pan. Puts it back on the flame. Burns the bottom.

Grace touches the tip of her tongue to the spoon and screams. "Why are you trying to scald me to death? Wicked, wicked girl." The bowl falls, shatters, splattering oatmeal everywhere. "Wicked, wicked girl you are." Sara's so angry she's close to tears.

"Oh, no. Oh, no," Grace murmurs. "What have I done

now? Oh, Sara Roberts. Sara Roberts. I'm so sorry. I never meant . . . I never did . . . It's my temper . . . it is . . . gets the better of me. Wouldn't you think after all these years? . . . But I've always had it . . . since I was a wee lass . . . a temper . . . a mean streak. I never mean to. I never do. It carries me off like a runaway horse." She looks up at Sara, her eyes like a child's—wide. "Sara, dear child, will you ever forgive me?"

"Sure." She wipes her eyes on her sleeve. "And I'm sorry. I really am. About this morning."

"Da was the only one who could do a thing with me when my temper took me for a spin. Me mother would throw up her hands in disgust. 'She's all yours,' she'd say, 'all yours.' "

"What did your Da do?"

"He'd bundle me up in something. An old quilt. Anything handy, and me kicking and squealing like some wild thing and him laughing and singing. That's what I remember best. Him laughing and singing. Until I quieted a bit. And then he'd settle me into his lap in a crook of his arm and he'd read to me awhile. Me Grimms'," she says shyly. She's found the ancient volume on the nightstand. She runs a finger gently down the binding.

"Would you like me to read to you, Grace? I wouldn't mind. I'd like to."

73

"Me Grimms'? No. You wouldn't like to. You're too old for fairy stories. Aren't you?"

"I wouldn't mind. Really, I wouldn't."

"And you don't think it too peculiar? An old thing like me?"

"No, I don't. I think it's fine," says Sara firmly. "I like them, too." This is not entirely true. It's been a long time since Sara has thought about fairy tales one way or another.

But in the end it turns out to be true. Because reading to Grace—day after day—she comes to love them. To honestly love them.

"So," says her mother, "how are Laura and Elizabeth doing?"

"Good, I guess."

"What have you kids been up to?" She's trying to keep it light. The strain shows.

"Not too much."

"How come?" She's smiling. And frowning.

"I don't know. I've been busy. You know. I've been trying to help around here. Like cutting the grass. And around the house." She knows as soon as she says it, it's a mistake.

"Oh, Sara. That's just what I thought. Just what I've been afraid of. Your summer's ruined. Because I have to work. It's all my fault. You're so pale, Sara. Are you getting out at all? I knew this would happen. Are you seeing Amy?"

"Not much. Amy's been hanging out with some other kids."

Her mother sighs. With relief? "Well, what do you do with yourself all day?"

"I don't know. Not much. I like being home. I like helping out. And I do get out. To see my friends . . . and I read a lot."

"I don't know, Sara. I really don't know what to think. I just can't help worrying."

"Oh, Mom, don't be so dour."

J uly.

August.

Sara reads a lot.

She learns to sing.

Maybe she could always sing, and it was only because she was told she couldn't that she couldn't. But anyway, she learns to sing.

Grace has a lovely voice. It isn't her speaking voice at all. That's gruff. And often sharp. And sometimes whiny.

Her singing voice is like her laugh. Soft and clear. Sweet.
Like a girl's.

The singing lessons begin with listening. That's harder
than it sounds. But slowly Sara learns to listen, to notice
the slight differences that make music. She listens and
then tries to follow. She makes mistakes. Grace doesn't
mind mistakes. "Try it again, lass. Try it again. Nothing
ventured, nothing gained."

Sara hates mistakes. They leave her feeling so awkward
and embarrassed. She wants to give it up, but Grace won't
let her.

Every now and then she finds the right note. Which
feels wonderful. She feels like singing. And the now-and-
thens come closer and closer. And she forgets she can't
sing, and she sings. And she finds the notes not one by one
but strings of notes—sweet, silvery strings. They sing
together. From the hymnal. And Grace teaches Sara the
songs of childhood. Old Scots tunes mostly. But "Go
Tell Aunt Rhodie," too, and "God Bless America."
"Kate Smith you're not," says Grace, "but you'll do."
Sara's never heard of Kate Smith, but she smiles and
blushes with pleasure.

"I guess you've heard about Amy," her father says.
"Uh-huh," she lies.
"What's this about Amy?" her mother asks.
Sara fills her mouth with mashed potatoes.

"Gone," says her father.

"Amy's gone?" says her mother. "Where? When?"

"Yesterday. Or the day before. I ran into Ted in the hardware store. . . . Sara, could you pass the butter? . . . Apparently the mother appeared out of nowhere. The West Coast, I think. Said she'd come for the kids. She missed them. And she was ready for them now. Ted says he asked the kids what they wanted to do. He expected the little boy to go with his mother. But Amy? Amy surprised him. They both took off with her. The same day. Just packed up and went."

"Poor Ted."

"Yeah. He looks terrible."

"He must be heartsick. He really loved . . . loves those kids."

Bitch, says Sara. To herself.

But Amy's not the one she's worried about. It's Grace.

Teaching Sara to sing had been good for her. Maybe it was the challenge. But more and more days are bad ones for Grace. The good ones are fewer and farther between. She's slipping, losing ground.

The confusion settles around her like a fog. She thinks

Sara is Helen. Mother. Da. People Sara's never heard of. Confusion thickens. She can't seem to shake it off like she used to. Sara's afraid that one day she'll disappear into that fog and never come back.

The commode's too much for her. She submits to the bedpan with hardly a whimper.

Her appetite's going. "I'm just not hungry today, Helen." Listlessly pushing the dish away. Or pouting like a spoiled child. "You never will cook anything nice. You know I hate this. You know I never like vegetables. The slimy things. You only make them to be mean."

Sara tries to coax her with vegetables from her father's garden. Green beans. Ripe tomatoes. And tiny, new potatoes with butter and parsley. Sometimes she takes a nibble or two before she throws the spoon down. "You're hateful," she says.

Sara says, "Good morning."
Grace doesn't move.
"Grace?"
She doesn't answer.
"Grace? What's the matter? Is anything wrong?"
"Go away. Leave me alone."
Sara turns to go. Hesitates. She has half a mind to walk out the door and never come back. Grace wouldn't care. Grace hates her. And she'd miss Grace. Oh, sure she'd

miss Grace. Like she misses her mother nagging her. Like she misses her "best friend," Amy. "Okay. If that's what you want, I'm going."

"Go."

"I'm going."

"Good." But she's crying. Sobbing into her pillow.

"Grace! What's the matter? I'm still here. Please tell me what's the matter."

"I've been bad. I've been so bad. I . . . I . . ."

"What's the matter, Grace? What did you do?"

Very, very softly. A whisper. "I wet."

Sara takes the sheets home to wash and dry them.

She makes the bed, stretching the clean sheets tight with hospital corners. Grace is sitting up. In the easy chair, with a blanket over her legs. It's the first time she's been out of bed for days. And she seems so much better. Cheerful. She even sings a little.

Settled back in bed, she yawns.

"Are you ready for a nap now, Grace? Shall I leave and come back a little later?"

Grace yawns again. And smiles. "A nap," she says. "Aye, that would be nice. A wee nap."

She dozes off, still smiling. But as Sara is softly opening the door, Grace cries out, "Sara?"

"What is it, Grace? I'm still here."

"Oh, I thought you'd gone. I thought . . . I must have dreamt it . . . I was all alone."

"Go back to sleep, Grace. It's okay. I'm right here."

"Aye. Good."

Snoring. Sara stays a few more minutes. Until she's sure Grace is sound asleep.

Her mother is sipping coffee, leafing through the morning paper. "David? Did you know Mrs. Craig died?"

"Oh, yes. Didn't I mention it? I heard it at the hospital. She never came into the hospital, though. I believe she died in her sleep at home."

"It says here the service is on Wednesday. I wonder if anyone will be there."

"I doubt it. She's lived like a hermit for as long as I can remember. I don't think she had a friend in the world."

"She has . . . had a daughter, though, didn't she? Out West somewhere?"

"Yeah, I think you're right. You would have thought the daughter would have taken some responsibility."

"David, do you think we should go to the service?"

"We hardly knew the woman."

"I know. . . ."

"Excuse me, please," says Sara.

She knew. She knew before she reached out—as if across a great distance—to touch Grace's hand. She can't remember all of it. She remembers holding the hand for a moment. As if to warm it. She remembers crying. For what seemed like a long, long time. Her face buried in the bedclothes. And hearing herself sob as if it were somebody else.

She hadn't gone back that afternoon. Or evening. Her mother's cousins from Nova Scotia had arrived—unexpected—and stayed for supper. And they sat around the table afterward, talking. And by the time the dishes were done, it was too late to run over and check on Grace.

She remembers seeing the Tenth curled up by Grace's feet. She remembers thinking, He doesn't know. He doesn't know. He thinks she's only sleeping.

She called the emergency number. Asked for an ambulance. "Someone's died. Mrs. Craig. Thirty-seven West Street."

"Cause of death?" The voice sounded bored. Another death.

"I don't know. I wasn't here. I guess she just died. She was old."

81

"People don't just die, honey. Who are you anyway?"

"I'm not anybody. A friend . . . of the family."

"We'll be right there. Stay where you are. Don't go anywhere."

She'd wanted to go. She couldn't let them find her there. She couldn't answer any questions. She'd wanted to go home. She wanted her mother. She wanted to feel her mother's arms around her.

But she'd stayed as long as she could. She couldn't leave Grace all alone again.

While she waited, she noticed on the nightstand the kind of cloth pocketbook women keep their knitting in. It hadn't been there yesterday. And with it was a note addressed to her. The handwriting was so faint she took it under the light to read it.

For Sara Roberts. For my dear friend. My Bible.
My hymns. My Grimms'. My pearl of great price.
Grace Craig. P.S. This is my will.

She heard the ambulance turn in the drive. She picked up the bag. It was heavy. Lifted the latch and slipped out back. The Tenth followed her across the garden.

Sara's riding her bike. She had to get out of the house. Thinking. Trying not to think.

Laura.

"Hi."

"Hi, Laura."

"How ya been?"

"Okay."

"Having a good summer?"

"Okay." Suddenly she sees Grace. Her face. Her eyes. Asking. Giving. She's afraid she'll cry.

"Listen, Sara . . . I'm really sorry . . . about what happened. I mean about telling and the police and all. I mean I know you probably don't believe me, but I really feel awful about it. Ever since I did it. I just wish I'd kept my big mouth shut." It's Laura now who's close to tears.

"It's okay. It doesn't matter. I'm not mad at you anymore. I never really was . . . mad at you. I guess I was really mad at me. It was my fault. The whole mess."

"Sara?"

"Yeah?"

"You want to do something together before school starts? Like go to the beach or something?"

"Yeah. I guess so. I mean, sure."

"And Elizabeth, too? If she can?"

"Sure . . . but she's probably too busy . . . mooning over Boy— I mean Rajah."

Laura smiles—broadly. "No, that's history. They had a big fight. Broke up. A long time ago. I don't think she's busy. It'd be fun. Like old times."

"Yeah," says Sara. "Like old times." She smiles.

She can't go into the church. She wants to, but she can't. Someone will ask who she is and what she wants. She waits in the shadow of the high shrubs that enclose the steps.

A woman walking her dog stares at her and keeps looking back over her shoulder, frowning. Sara pretends she's looking for something in the bushes.

It's so quiet in there. Like a tomb. There's no music. She thought there was always music at funerals. Probably Helen hates music. Or she's too busy for it. In too much of a hurry to catch a plane or something.

The heavy doors open. They straggle out.

First a woman in a dark suit. Felt hat and veil. Several strands of pearls. Helen. Sara can't see a face through the netting. But the way she walks, the way she holds her head, she doesn't seem sorry . . . or sad. But maybe she is. Sara wonders how she would feel if this were her mother's funeral.

A few old people. A woman leaning heavily on a cane. No one Sara recognizes, except the minister.

At the cemetery, beyond the grave, a couple of men in overalls lean on their shovels.

Sara pretends she's just out for a walk. She studies a gravestone.

"Our beloved sister . . ."

"Ashes to ashes . . ."

"In sure and certain hope . . ."

Over. So quickly. They're shaking hands. Like a business deal.

Helen walks away briskly. And into a taxi waiting at the curb.

Sara touches the pearl under her jersey. She wonders if Helen looked for it. Probably not. She has plenty of pearls. But she must have known about it. Thought it was for her. Probably she thought it was lost. Or stolen. Well, it wasn't. Sara had the paper. Locked in her desk drawer.

The woman at the farm remembers her. She's very kind. "Of course, dear. Take what you like. Do you need any help?"

"No, thank you. I'll be fine."

Sara leans her bike against a tree.

She digs out a shoot of white lilac. Deep and deeper she digs until she strikes a ledge. She wraps the root ball in newspaper, ties it, and soaks it under the hose.

Climbing, she doesn't think about anything. She just climbs. It's a cool morning. The sun is bright, but already it seems thinner. A September sun. It's windy on top. She shivers. September. Almost September.

She finds a large, flat stone. With her father's camping knife she carves it. G R A C E. Good. Grace would approve. Plain. Nothing fancy.

She plants the lilac. It may make it. But it will have to be tough. And it will need some luck. Rain. And a long, mild season.

It's over.

It's time to go home.

There's McTavish the Tenth to see to.

Her mother won't stand for it. Won't have him in the house.

But when she hears the whole story . . .

It's time the whole story was told.

The time for lies and secrets . . . that time is over, too.

They'll listen. They always listen. And they'll understand.

It's very still. Sara listens. Listens until she can hear Grace's song. And then she joins in. Their song rises on the wind. Floating out over the valleys.

"Amazing Grace, how sweet the sound . . .

That saved a wretch like me . . ."

Rising and floating out over the valleys. And an echo. Like an answer.

"I once was lost, but now am found . . ."

A woman kneels in the damp spring earth. Her cat rubs against her, purring. She's setting lilac cuttings.

"Was blind, but now I see."

He lifts his little daughter higher.

Higher . . . until she's astride the drafter's broad back.

Laughing,

    he tells her

        she looks like a queen.

About the Author

Liesel Moak Skorpen was born in Germany and grew up in Ohio. After graduation from Wells College, she studied philosophy at Yale on a Woodrow Wilson Scholarship.

Although Grace is her first book for older readers, Ms. Skorpen is the author of many well-known picture books, among them ELIZABETH, CHARLES, and HIS MOTHER'S DOG. She and her famly live in Verona Island, Maine, where she enjoys riding and showing her thoroughbred Percheron horse, Abby.